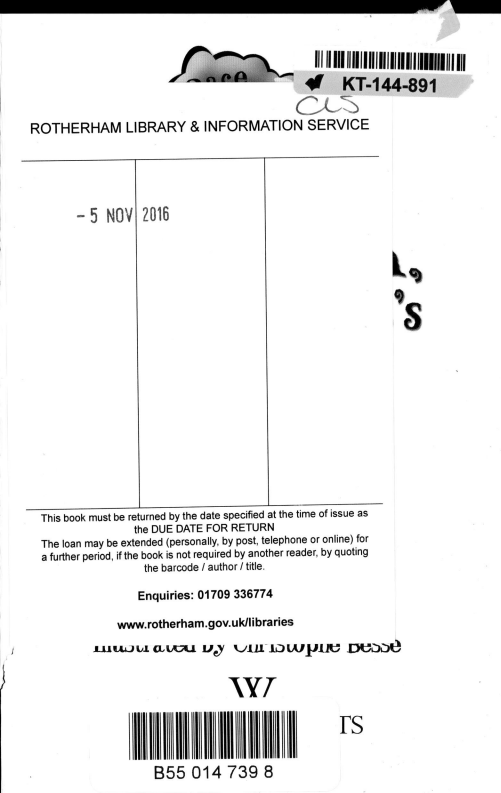

KT-144-891

CLS

ROTHERHAM LIBRARY & INFORMATION SERVICE

- 5 NOV 2016	

Illustrated by Christophe Besse

W

TS

Meet the Scatterbrains

Lancelot Scatterbrain

Tom Scatterbrain

Queen Rose

CHAPTER 1
Knight School

"Ready your arrows!" ordered Mr Galahad, the head of Knight School. Today's class was on archery. "Now draw your bow!" Mr Galahad called. Agnes, the only girl in the class, took an arrow from her quiver and aimed at the target.

"Wait!" shouted Mr Galahad when he spotted Lancelot. As usual, Lancelot Scatterbrain was running late.

"I'm sorry, Sir. I got lost," he panted.

Lancelot was the son of Sir Tom Scatterbrain, and Prince of Luckless Castle.

Being a bit of a scatterbrain had run in
the family for a long time now. A true
Scatterbrain would always go left when
advised to go right, his dad had told him.
Lancelot stood next to Agnes.

"Hello, Lancelot."

"Hello, Agnes."

"Today," said Agnes, "I'm going to hit the bullseye! I've made a special arrow with the feathers from a parrot. It's very colourful!"

"It's beautiful! Could I borrow one?" Lancelot asked.

"I left all mine at the castle."

Agnes smiled and handed him a black-feathered arrow.

"Is everyone ready?" Mr Galahad asked.

"Draw your bows!"

Lancelot was holding the bow all wrong.

"Stop, Lancelot!" Mr Galahad called out.

The young knight turned round with
his bow and arrow still raised.

"Help! Everyone duck!" the teacher yelled.
"Lancelot, how many times have I told you
not to point your arrow at anyone?"

Just then, a bird distracted Lancelot and he carelessly pointed his bow upwards.
"Ready. Aim. Shoot!" ordered the teacher.

Lancelot's arrow shot straight up to the sky.

Agnes's shot was not much better and her arrow flew off into the forest.
"Remember you're aiming for the target, you two!" the teacher cried.

"I'll go and get my arrow," Agnes sighed.

"Don't even think about it!"

warned Mr Galahad.

"No one who goes into Deadwood Forest ever comes back! Witches, dragons and all sorts of creepy monsters live there!"

Later on, everyone was gathered round the table for their mid-morning snack when Mr Galahad suddenly asked: "Where's Agnes?" Then he shook as he realised that she'd gone into the forest.

CHAPTER 2
In Deadwood Forest

Pushing through leaves and ferns, Lancelot made his way through the forest. He knew just how mad Mr Galahad would be to discover that another of his students had disappeared, but he had to help Agnes!

Lancelot spotted a piece of fabric hanging
from a bush. It was a piece of Agnes's dress.
Just then, a voice spoke in rhyme:
"*Knight, have you lost your way?*
Who do you seek now anyway?"

Lancelot turned round. In front of him stood a very tall old man, a wizard, dressed in white.

Lancelot replied bravely:

"I'm looking for a princess who lost her arrow. Have you seen her?"

The wizard spoke in rhyme again:

"I have seen no one but you

For hours, days and whole months too!

But who are you, my young brave knight,

To enter these woods in broad daylight?"

"I am Lancelot Scatterbrain,

Prince of Luckless Castle."

The wizard continued:

"A princess and the heir to a throne

Both lost in the forest, all alone.

Beware, if Spelleanor should find thee

In terrible danger you will be."

"What are you talking about? Who's Spelleanor?" asked Lancelot nervously.

"She's an evil sorceress on her broom,

Who brings this place nothing but gloom.

There are two paths by a lime tree,

A few hundred metres behind me.

The path on your left you must take,

For your princess's life is now at stake."

Lancelot hurried on, but when he turned round, the wizard had vanished. Soon he reached the lime tree with two paths, just as the wizard had described.

"Now," Lancelot thought, "what did the wizard say? Don't go left. Take the right path. Yes, I'm sure that was it." So Lancelot went deeper and deeper into Deadwood Forest.

CHAPTER 3
The Magic Potion

At last, Lancelot reached a clearing and saw
an old woman dressed in rags. Suddenly
there was a flash of light. When he looked
again, the woman had changed and she
was holding a broom.

"Hello, I am looking for a lost princess. Have you seen her?" Lancelot said.

Then he remembered the wizard's warning about the evil sorceress.

"Are you the sorceress who lives in the forest?'" he asked, worried.

"Who, me?" she replied, shocked.

"No, I'm just a little old fairy."

She wore a white dress but it was tattered
and her hat was old. She had straw-coloured
hair and little fairy wings.

"Who are you looking for?" she asked.

"A princess called Agnes,"
Lancelot stuttered.

"She's about my height–"

"Oh yes, I did see her!" the fairy interrupted.
"But I'm afraid I have bad news."

"What's happened?" Lancelot asked.

"She was captured by the dragon – it took her to its lair. You'll have to act fast to rescue her," the fairy told him.

"Then I must go!" Lancelot cried.
"Stop! You'll need help to fight the
dragon and escape from this cursed
forest. I can make a magic potion to
help you find a way out. But first I need
these missing ingredients." She read out
a list of ingredients from a parchment:

1. *The stem of a fern*

2. *Half a litre of rainwater*

3. *A scale from a dead dragon*

4. *A princess's nail clipping*

5. *A handful of knight's hair, burned*
    by the flames of a dragon.

"I don't have the dragon's scale…" began the fairy.

"Then let me bring it to you!" proposed Lancelot proudly.

"I also need a princess's nail clipping," she said, and smiled a wicked smile.

"Follow me. I'll lead you to the dragon's lair." Lancelot didn't realise that the fairy was in fact Spelleanor, the evil sorceress.

CHAPTER 4
The Dragon's Lair

Spelleanor led Lancelot further into the forest until they reached a cliff. Then she whispered in Lancelot's ear: "Here we are, young knight. See the opening in the rocks over there? That's the dragon's lair."

"Let's go!" Lancelot shouted.

"Wait a minute!" Spelleanor stopped him.

"A dragon isn't easy to defeat. Count ten steps towards the lair and chant: 'I am not scared of your flames, little dragon!' This spell will protect you from the fire," she lied.

"But really it will wake the dragon up!"

she laughed to herself.

"Then you will be toast!

I'll get a handful of knight's

 hair as well as your princess's

nail clipping, you stupid

little knight!"

Lancelot checked

his weapons.

"I have my bow,

but I forgot my

arrows..."

he realised.

"Follow my advice, then you won't need any arrows to fight the dragon!" lied the evil sorceress. Ahead of Lancelot, the entrance to the lair looked like a gaping hole ready to gobble him up! He counted his steps: "One, two, three, four and five. I am not scared of your games, little dra…"

28

"No!" Spelleanor interrupted him.

"I told you to count to ten. And that

isn't the right sentence! Try again!"

Lancelot tried it again and counted ten steps.

He took a deep breath and boomed:

"I am not scared of your names, little..."

"No, no, no!" Spelleanor was angry now.

"Those words are all wrong!" She repeated

the correct words again. But, like a true

Scatterbrain, Lancelot could not get it right.

Spelleanor pushed Lancelot in front of the

entrance to

the lair.

"It's easy. Just count ten steps from here. Look, I'll show you. Then you say: 'I am not scared of your flames, little dragon!'" All of a sudden, an enormous green shape emerged from the cave.

The gigantic dragon breathed out huge flames. Lancelot stepped back and shielded his face. When he looked up, he saw a small pile of ashes where Spelleanor had stood seconds earlier.

Then he saw the recipe for the magic potion. He realised that the fairy had been trying to trick him into being burned by the dragon. The fairy had actually been Spelleanor all along.

Suddenly a voice called out from inside the cave. "Help! Help!" Agnes cried.

Lancelot saw Agnes trapped behind the dragon. She was holding her colourful arrow – at least she had found it! Lancelot reached for his quiver, then remembered he had no arrows…

CHAPTER 5
The Final Challenge!

The dragon's red eyes stared at Lancelot.
It lifted its head up and roared. Lancelot
raised his bow bravely, forgetting he had
no arrows left.

Meanwhile, Agnes had managed to get out of the lair and stood by Lancelot's side. As the dragon prepared to fill its lungs and breathe out fire, there was a strange whizzing noise.

Agnes and Lancelot watched an arrow zoom over them...

...and land right in the dragon's head!

Defeated, the dragon collapsed.

"It's the arrow I shot earlier!" Lancelot said as he recognised the black feathers. "I fired it accidentally in class this morning."

He removed the arrow and put it back in his quiver. Then he took the princess's hand. "Let's go home now. Everyone must be worried." As they walked back towards the edge of the forest, they both told each other their stories.

"The old wizard led me to the sorceress,

who then gave me to the dragon," Agnes

explained.

"And the wizard tried to lead me away from

you," said Lancelot. "He knew that together,

we could beat Spelleanor."

Just then the wizard magically appeared in front of them. Agnes could feel her anger rising inside her. "You again!" she roared. "You and your stupid rhymes!"

"Did you fight with all your might
And beat the dragon without a weapon?"
the wizard asked.

"You could say so," Lancelot replied. "But we can't thank you for that!"

"Guarding the forest is my mission,

No one leaves without my permission!" the wizard chanted.

"We'll see about that!' Lancelot said, while Agnes snatched the bow from his hands. She hit the wizard on the head with the bow and he fell to the floor.

"Don't you think I've improved at archery?" she giggled and they both burst out laughing.

"How will we get out of the forest?"

Agnes asked.

"We could use this," said Lancelot, pulling

the magic potion recipe out of his pocket.

"Great! We have all the ingredients ... except

a dragon's scale. Can you remember the

way to the lair?"Agnes asked Lancelot.

Lancelot shook his head, but he had
an idea.

He reached inside his quiver for his only arrow. "I could shoot this arrow in the sky again and it may lead to the dragon?" Agnes stared at the arrow in amazement. "You're a genius, my brave knight! Look!"

Looking down at the arrow, Lancelot saw that a dragon's scale was still firmly attached to its tip.

A thunderstorm rumbled nearby.

"I think it's time to go home!" Agnes said with a smile, knowing it was about to rain.

Night was falling when Lancelot and Agnes reached the edge of the forest, where the magic potion had transported them. They were greeted by the sound of excited cries from the other side of the bushes.

Mr Galahad and the rest of the class cheered. King Alistair and Queen Beatrice, Agnes's parents, hugged her tightly. Lancelot's mother, Queen Rose, greeted her son. She had wanted to come in person, despite her tummy being as round as the moon. She was expecting a new royal baby!

"We were so worried!" Queen Rose told Lancelot. He looked at the crowd around him. "Where's Dad?" he asked.

"As soon as he heard of your disappearance, he jumped on his horse and raced to the rescue." replied his mother.

"But we didn't see him," said Lancelot.

"That's because he went to Dearwood Forest instead of Deadwood Forest!" said Queen Rose.

Queen Rose sighed. "Scatterbrains run first and think later, both father and son."

"Well as far as love's arrow goes, this Scatterbrain knows how to aim!" Agnes said. She leaned towards Lancelot and kissed him on the lips. Lancelot's cheeks turned bright red as Agnes spoke in rhyme:

"My dearest knight, so brave and true,

I give this loving kiss to you.

With your bow and arrow bold,

My dear love you'll always hold!"

Franklin Watts
First published in Great Britain in 2015 by
The Watts Publishing Group

© RAGEOT-EDITEUR Paris, 2010
First published in French as
Le Fils Du Chevalier Têtenlère

Translation © Franklin Watts 2015
English text and adaptation by Fabrice
Blanchefort.

Series Editor: Melanie Palmer
Series Advisor: Catherine Glavina
Cover Designer: Cathryn Gilbert
Design Manager: Peter Scoulding

ISBN 978 1 4451 3730 8 (hbk)
ISBN 978 1 4451 3733 9 (pbk)
ISBN 978 1 4451 3731 5 (ebook)
ISBN 978 1 4451 3732 2 (library ebook)

Printed in China

MIX
Paper from
responsible sources
FSC® C104740
FSC
www.fsc.org

Franklin Watts
An imprint of
Hachette Children's Group
Part of The Watts Publishing Group
Carmelite House
50 Victoria Embankment
London EC4Y 0DZ

An Hachette UK Company
www.hachette.co.uk

www.franklinwatts.co.uk